This is a Magabala Book

LEADING PUBLISHER OF ABORIGINAL AND
TORRES STRAIT ISLANDER STORYTELLERS.

CHANGING THE WORLD, ONE STORY AT A TIME.

First published 2020, reprinted 2021
Magabala Books Aboriginal Corporation
1 Bagot Street, Broome, Western Australia
Website: www.magabala.com
Email: sales@magabala.com

Magabala Books receives financial assistance from the Commonwealth Government through the Australia Council, its arts advisory body. The State of Western Australia has made an investment in this project through the Department of Local Government, Sport and Cultural Industries. Magabala Books would like to acknowledge the generous support of the Shire of Broome, Western Australia.

Magabala Books is Australia's only independent Aboriginal and Torres Strait Islander publishing house. Magabala Books acknowledges the Traditional Owners of the Country on which we live and work. We recognise the unbroken connection to traditional lands, waters and cultures. Through what we publish, we honour all our Elders, peoples and stories, past, present and future.

Translation from English to Gija by Eileen Bray
Gija language editor Frances Kofod

Endpapers feature (front left and back right) Skin group from my father's mother's side, 2018 by Shirley Purdie
(front right and back left) Skin group from my mother's side, 2018 by Shirley Purdie

Editing, cover and internal design Cathie Tasker and Deborah Brown
Printed in China by Everbest Printing Company

GOVERNMENT OF WESTERN AUSTRALIA
KIMBERLEY DEVELOPMENT COMMISSION

The Kimberley Art Centre Series is an outcome of the Kimberley Art Centre Project, which was supported by funding from the State Government of Western Australia and the Oranges and Sardines Foundation.

Cataloguing-in-Publication data available from the National Library of Australia

NATIONAL LIBRARY OF AUSTRALIA
A catalogue record for this book is available from the National Library of Australia

Department of Local Government, Sport and Cultural Industries
lotterywest supported
Australian Government
Australia Council for the Arts
Shire of Broome

Shirley Purdie

Ngaginybe Jarragbe
My Story

Gija translation by Eileen Bray

Magabala Books

I am Shirley Purdie.

A long time ago
my mother danced
with the women at Mabel Downs.
The men made music.

Happy times.

Ngayindi Birrmarriyan-nga.

Warna-warnarram
ngaginyel gooral warrg nyanini-berrab
yagengerram ngalingalim Gilban.
Jiyilembi dam ngalany berrani-boorroo.

Gooloo-gooloowoom.

I was born at Mabel Downs.
We call that place Gilban.

My dreaming is echidna dreaming
and fire dreaming.
My father looked into the fire
and saw an echidna.

That's why.

Ngayindi bedalg ngenewardge Gilban.

Ngaginybe goonim gernanyjel
doo marnem.
Ngagenyji ngaboony deg nginini marnen
gedba nyaniyidji dal gernanyjel.

Wayinigana.

My mother's country is Baluwah
(Violet Valley).

Three women roll spinifex
near where the barramundi
jumped through the gap in the hills.
See them there.

Ngaginyel gooral-ngooyoo daam Baloowa.

Merrgernbem ngalim gerlgayi berrani-gili
gerlerne-baya
daan ngirriban dal dayiwool
jarrg-ngarri nyaneward doomboon.

Deg gala bamberrem.

My mother shows me how to find bushtucker. When the time is right this tree is yellow with flowers.

That's when we dig.

Ngaginyel gooral jirriji ngenamanya deg-girrim gibingarnam-boorroo mayim. Jamoonin menkawoom. Ngelela goonjal thawalam goorndoorl-ba waniyidja-ngarri.

Wayiniyana jarrij yirrarn.

My mother, my aunty and grandmother are kind.
When the school teacher gets kangaroo ticks
they pick them out of her.

Those ticks make you sore ... and red.

Ngaginyel gooral, gawangel doo ganggal menkawoom-gili.
Dal lendijgalel loorrma-loorrma-ba-ngarri waniyid
Denggij bemberramangbe-ngiyi.

Damga loorrma-loorrma gajig namberrimnha-boorroo, galimbirreg.

Women use the bark of
the freshwater mangrove
to make a soapy lather
to kill and catch the fish.
The lather doesn't hurt people.

We eat that fish.

*Ngali-ngalim nyaj ngoorroomenbe
dany mangoonyji
nyoomarlig dambi goorloom
thedji-girrim dam goorndarrim.
Ngoowan warrernbeg
yimberremenbe-yoowoo
nyoomarlim dam.*

Jang yirramande dambi goorndarrim.

I'm a girl and this bush orange tree is a girl.
Boys can't say her name.

But they can eat her fruit.

Ngayin-ga ngalin-nga, dali-miyi joogoorrool ngalin-nyaliny.
Jambalngarri-woorrarrem ngoowan garij nyimberremenbe yinginybe-ngiyi.

Menkawoom jang-gan.

We go out to get bush honey
and cut it out of the tree.

We eat that sugarbag.

Marra yirradji gibi-yoorroong
ngarem-boorroo.
Lawoog yirremenji goowoole-biny.

Jang yirrarn dambi ngarem.

My mum would go off to work.

I stay home with the animals –
one pussycat, one galah,
one little black dog
and a joey kangaroo.

They are my mates.

Ngaginyel gooral marra nyaninyande
warrgam-girrem.
Ngayindi daan ngenaniyinde.
ngirrngili-baya, gerliny-gerliny-baya,
wanyageny manbeny joola-baya,
woonggare-baya.

Birriyama ngagenybe jarlijim.

One day I go with my grandmother
to look for a nanny goat near Yallanji river.
One of our dogs finds something in a cave.
It is a kangaroo.

That kangaroo becomes our dinner.

Ngayin ngenayin-ngiyiwa ngaginyel ganggal
Yalan-yoorroong biya-wiya-girrim
miyinggajim-boorroo.
Jirrawoony joolany bilij nginiyidji jiyirriny
yiligin nawane.

Jang yirrani dany jiyirriny.

I worked as a maid on Mabel Downs Station.

I wake up at dawn and work all day.
I work hard and can't stop until
I have washed up all the dishes after dinner.

The days are long.

Warrgam ngenani Gilban.

Berdij ngenayinde rangarrwayan warrgam
ngelamande wayiniya mendoowoony.
Ngoowan ngarrij ngenaniyin
warrgam ngelemande loogoorr
noonemangge jaboogoom girrij

Dirrandem merewam.

My mother showed me how to get bushtucker
and she showed me how to paint.
Her name was Madigan Thomas.

A long time ago my uncle Jack Britten said to me, 'Why don't you try yourself for painting, you might be all right.'

The Warmun artists and Rover Thomas and Queenie McKenzie inspired me.

It was hard learning all I needed to know.

Ngaginyel gooral jirriji ngenamanyande gibi-ngarnam mayim. Binarrig ngenamanya nyoon-nyoon-girrem.

Yinginybe-ngiyi Jawoodjil.

Warna-warnarram ngaginyji nyaganyji Yalarrji wanema-ngirri "Gool gala biyilij nyoon-nyoon-girrem, menkawoon-anyji-ngoo.

Bagarrjim berrani-ngirri nyoon-girrembi lingawa ngenawardge, binarriwa ngelayidge.

I sold my first painting and got better and better ... and now I'm a famous artist. My paintings are all over the world hanging in important places.

I'm still painting, sharing corroboree, hunting for bushtucker and teaching the young people.

Happy times.

Gelengiyana nyoon-nyoon-ngarri ngenani berra niniyidge ngarrgalem-boorroo.
Men'ga-men'gawoo ngelida.
Ngayindi gelengendi nawarram-ngirri yinginybe nyoon-nyoon-girrem.

Dambi nyoon-nyoon-ngarri noonamangge berra bemberrayidbe ngoorroo-ngoorroon ngirribawoorroon Dardard boorroonboo daan nawarran.

Nyoon-nyoon ngelemen'gende jimerrawoon.
Binarrig noonemen'ge wanyanyagem
Joonbam-boorroo, gibi-ngarnam-boorroo mayim.

Gooloo-gooloowoom.

Shirley Purdie

The author

Shirley Purdie has been painting for more than twenty years and is an artist of increasing significance and seniority. Her cultural knowledge and artistic skill complement each other to produce a practice that holds great strength. Shirley is also a prominent leader in Warmun community and an incisive cross-cultural communicator.

Inspired by more senior Warmun artists including her late mother, the great Madigan Thomas, as well as Rover Thomas and Queenie McKenzie, Shirley began to paint her Country in the early 1990s. Shirley's uncle, artist Jack Britten, said to her, 'Why don't you try yourself for painting, you might be all right.'

Shirley says, 'It's good to learn from old people. They keep saying when you paint you can remember that Country, just like to take a photo, but there's the Ngarranggarni (Dreaming) and everything. Good to put it in painting, your Country, so kids can know and understand. When the old people die, young people can read the stories from the paintings. They can learn from the paintings and maybe they want to start painting too.' Shirley's body of work explores sites and narratives associated with the Country of her mother and father and is characterised by a bold use of richly textured ochre.

Significant places such as Baloowa, Jirragin and Gilban lie on Country now taken in by Violet Valley and Mabel Downs cattle stations. Much of her work also explores spirituality and the relationship between Gija conceptions of Ngarranggarni (Dreaming) and Catholicism. In 2007 Shirley was awarded the Blake Prize for Religious Art for her major work Stations of the Cross. Colonial histories of the region also figure in Shirley's work in which she relates accounts of early contact, massacre, warfare and indentured labour since the incursion of pastoralists into Gija land in the late 1800s.

Shirley is presently working on a major exhibition and publication of great cultural and ecological value, documenting through painting and in Gija language, the plants and trees of her Country.

The exhibition

Ngalim-Ngalimbooroo Ngagenybe was created for the 2018 National Portrait Gallery exhibition So Fine: Contemporary women artists make Australian history, in which curators Dr Sarah Engledow and Christine Clark invited ten artists to reflect on and reinterpret Australian history through contemporary portraiture. In September 2019 the series of 36 paintings by Shirley Purdie was acquired for the Gallery's collection, an acknowledgment of Purdie's personal history as a crucial part of the Australian experience, and one that will become increasingly important in the national conversation around cultural life and national identity.

Ngalim-Ngalimbooroo Ngagenybe 2018 by Shirley Purdie. Collection: National Portrait Gallery, Australia. © Shirley Purdie.

Warmun Art Centre

Warmun Art Centre is a non-profit Aboriginal Corporation situated in Warmun Aboriginal Community (previously Turkey Creek), off the Great Northern Highway, and around 200km south of Kununurra. It is a 100% Gija-owned and controlled community enterprise, world-renowned for its fine Aboriginal art featuring locally sourced ochre. The income made from sales of Warmun artworks is split between artists and the centre, with the centre's proceeds reinvested in operational needs that serve the artists and community.

Established in 1998, Warmun Art Centre quickly achieved local and international recognition, thanks to the leadership and guidance of successful predecessors including the late artists Rover Thomas, Queenie McKenzie, George Mung Mung and Paddy Jaminji. The distinctive Warmun style of art continues to inspire a new generation of Warmun artists who represent Gija art and culture with bold character and exciting diversity. The Art Centre also boasts a range of programs that carry on the legacy of the first wave of Elders and cultural practitioners. These include employment programs for remote Indigenous arts workers, a Joonba (corroboree) program, cultural learning programs and language revitalisation projects. The Art Centre is proudly funded by both Federal and State governments in its key program areas.

Magabala Books and The Series

Based in Broome, Western Australia, Magabala Books is Australia's leading Indigenous publishing house. Aboriginal-owned and controlled, Magabala publishes Aboriginal and Torres Strait Islander storytellers, authors and illustrators in all genres, from all over Australia. Magabala is renowned for its program of professional development and the Kimberley Art Centre Series is one such program.

The Kimberley Art Centre Series focuses on developing the skills of Kimberley Aboriginal artists in children's picture book storytelling and illustration. Begun in 2017, with illustration workshops across the Kimberley, Magabala has worked with artists and art centres to develop a series of children's picture books telling local Kimberley stories. *Shirley Purdie, My Story* is the first publication in the series. The project is generously supported by the State Government of Western Australia's Kimberley Development Commission through a Regional Economic Development Grant.

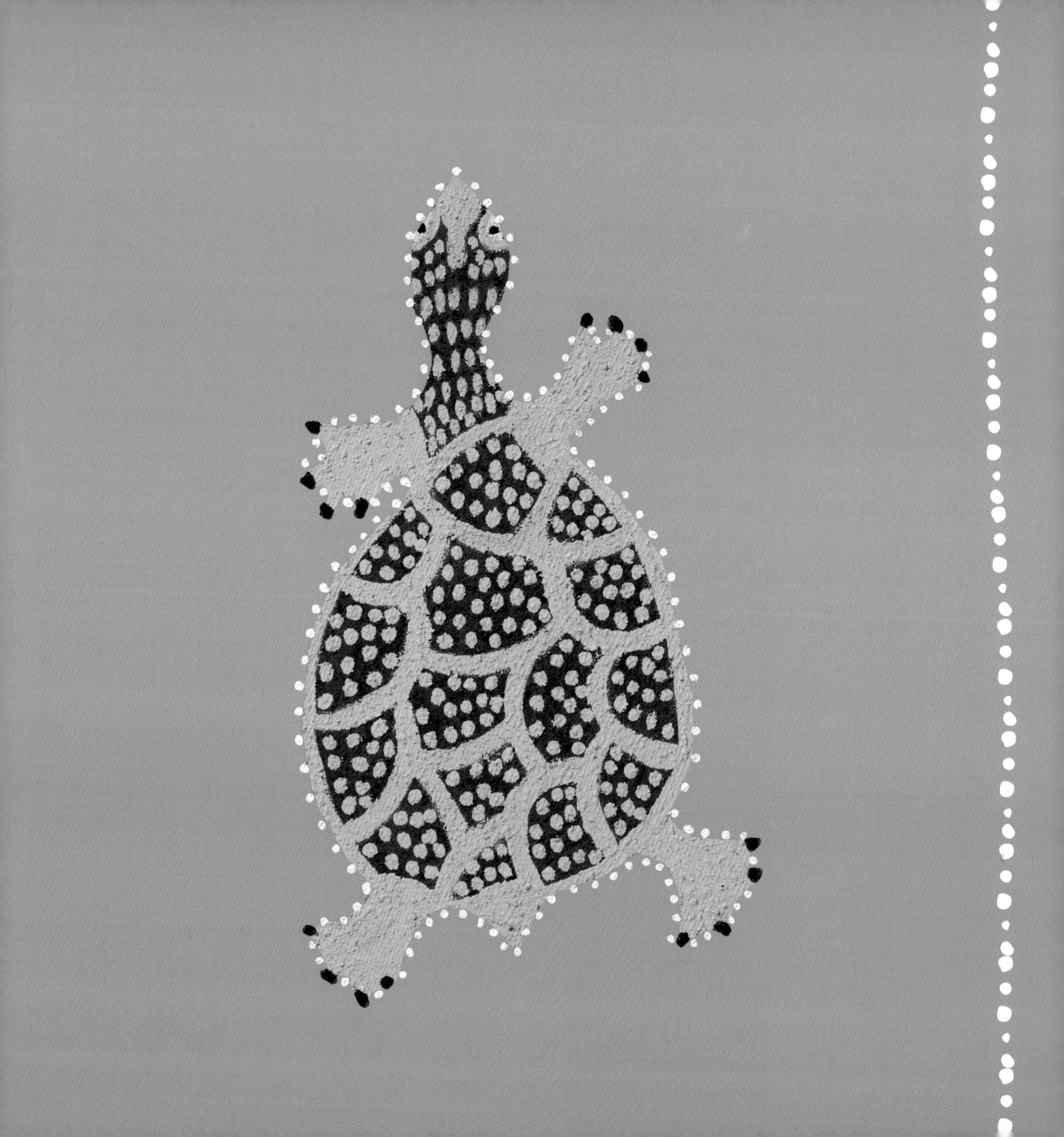